Beach Buddies

Puffin Books

Juliet
nearly a Vet

Beach Buddies

REBECCA JOHNSON

Illustrated by Kyla May

Puffin Books

PUFFIN BOOKS

Published by the Penguin Group
Penguin Group (Australia)
707 Collins Street, Melbourne, Victoria 3008, Australia
(a division of Penguin Australia Pty Ltd)
Penguin Group (USA) Inc.
375 Hudson Street, New York, New York 10014, USA
Penguin Group (Canada)
90 Eglinton Avenue East, Suite 700, Toronto, Canada ON M4P 2Y3
(a division of Penguin Canada Books Inc.)
Penguin Books Ltd
80 Strand, London WC2R 0RL England
Penguin Ireland
25 St Stephen's Green, Dublin 2, Ireland
(a division of Penguin Books Ltd)
Penguin Books India Pvt Ltd
11 Community Centre, Panchsheel Park, New Delhi – 110 017, India
Penguin Group (NZ)
67 Apollo Drive, Rosedale, Auckland 0632, New Zealand
(a division of Penguin New Zealand Pty Ltd)
Penguin Books (South Africa) (Pty) Ltd
Rosebank Office Park, Block D,
181 Jan Smuts Avenue, Parktown North, Johannesburg, 2196, South Africa
Penguin (Beijing) Ltd
7F, Tower B, Jiaming Center, 27 East Third Ring Road North,
Chaoyang District, Beijing 100020, China

Penguin Books Ltd, Registered Offices: 80 Strand, London, WC2R 0RL, England

First published by Penguin Group (Australia), 2014

1 3 5 7 9 10 8 6 4 2

Text copyright © Rebecca Johnson, 2014
Illustrations copyright © Kyla May Productions, 2014

Cover and text design by Karen Scott © Penguin Group (Australia)
Illustrations by Kyla May Productions
Typeset in New Century Schoolbook
Colour separation by Splitting Image Colour Studio, Clayton, Victoria
Printed and bound in Australia by Griffin Press, an accredited ISO AS/NZS 14001
Environmental Management Systems printer.

National Library of Australia
Cataloguing-in-Publication data:

Johnson, Rebecca.
Beach Buddies/Rebecca Johnson; illustrated by Kyla May.

ISBN: 978 0 14 330824 9 (pbk.)

A823.4

puffin.com.au

Hi! I'm Juliet. I'm ten years old.
And I'm nearly a vet!

I bet you're wondering how someone who is only ten
could nearly be a vet. It's pretty simple really.
My mum's a vet. I watch what she does and
I help out all the time. There's really not that
much to it, you know...

For my Neil,
for always being there.

XX R

CHAPTER 1

Vets never stop being vets

'*Come on*, Juliet, or we'll be setting up
the tent in the dark!'

I can hear that Dad's starting to
lose his cool.

'Coming,' I call as I try to stuff a
couple more things into my vet kit
that used to be Dad's fishing box.
I manage to snap one clip closed but
the other just won't budge.

I stagger out the front door with my
load, and the look of horror on Dad's
face says it all. The car is packed to

the roof in the back and there's not much room left.

'No way! You are not bringing all that with you,' says Dad, shaking his head.

My best friend Chelsea is on her way over from her house next door. She's coming camping with us and we're so excited. She's got a neat little backpack that takes up about a quarter of the space mine does, but most of my gear is vet equipment. You never know what emergencies might come up on a trip, so I have to be prepared for anything.

'Don't worry, Dad,' I say soothingly. 'It can all go under our feet. I like having my feet up in the car.'

'And where's the dog going to sit?'

'On my lap, of course!'

'Juliet, it's a four-hour trip. The dog is not going to just lie on your lap happily the whole time.'

'He can sit on mine, too,' Chelsea pipes up helpfully.

'And mine,' says Max, trying to open a lollipop and hold three dinosaurs at once.

'Fine, suit yourselves. But I don't want to hear any whingeing.'

'Who's whingeing?' says Mum as she pulls the front door closed.

'No one, yet . . .' grumbles Dad.

We haven't even made it out of

our street before poor Curly breaks wind. It must be the excitement of coming on holidays with us. I look over at Chelsea and I can see her eyes starting to water as she desperately tries to breathe through her shirt.

Max howls with laughter. I'll never really understand the way boys think.

We start playing I-spy and the alphabet game, but we're sick of that after twenty minutes.

'Did you bring your grooming kit, Chelsea?'

'Of course,' says Chelsea, patting the bag at her feet. 'Although I'm not sure there will be many animals to groom at the beach.'

'I guess you can always practise on Curly.'

Max has fallen asleep sucking a lollipop. His mouth is hanging open and the lollipop is in danger of falling out, so I place one of his dinosaurs under his chin to prop it shut. Curly is panting in my face and wagging his tail in Chelsea's, so it's getting pretty squashy. Every now and then Dad looks into the back at us and we try our best to look like we are having a very comfortable time. I can see he's just waiting for us to whinge, but it's not going to happen.

'Did you bring your vet kit, Mum?' I say.

'No, honey, I didn't. I'm on holidays and there will be vet surgeries nearby if an animal's in trouble.'

I look at Chelsea and we both shake our heads and I roll my eyes. Mum should know better. A vet never knows when an emergency is going to happen.

Curly eventually lies down and goes to sleep and I'm able to reach my Vet Diary from my bag. Chelsea and I start to make a list of the animals we might see on a beach camping holiday.

Seagulls
Fish
Pelicans
Crabs
Dolphins

When we finally drive into the campground it's well after lunch. It's taken us longer because Max threw up (Mum thinks he overdid it on the lollies) and Dad kept stopping to let Curly out to see if he needed to go to the toilet after a few too many really bad smells.

I can see Chelsea is nearly weeping tears of joy when Mum says we're here.

'Don't go wandering off too far, or near the water,' says Mum. 'We'll need you to help us carry all the stuff into the tent once we get it set up.'

The best thing is Curly gets to sleep in the tent with us. Our tent is really

big and has two separate rooms. Chelsea,
Max, Curly and I have one room, and
Mum and Dad are in the other.

We race off to explore. The camping
ground is amazing. We've only just
arrived and I could already fill a whole

page with the animals we've seen. I can't wait to explore the rock pools and beach this afternoon. Vets need to know about all kinds of animals because vets are vets, even when they are on holidays.

CHAPTER 2

Vets need to be kind to all animals

We set our beds up in the tent. Chelsea's going to sleep on the air bed in the middle between Max and me. She spends ages making her bed really neat and even has a little cushion and some soft toys. Max hasn't got his sleeping bag out yet, but he has arranged his dinosaurs all around the edges of the tent.

'They're going to get in the way, Max,' I say, swiping a few aside.

'Hey!' whines Max. 'Don't hit them!' He crawls straight over Chelsea's neat bed to pick them up.

'Why did you have to bring so many dinosaurs anyway?' I grumble.

I make room for my vet kit, my emergency rescue pack (this has some extra things for special situations that I wouldn't normally carry in my vet kit, like Grandad's old binoculars), and my pet carrier, which I also brought in case of an emergency.

꙳

When we're all set up and Chelsea has re-made her bed, it's time to go to the beach. We take off, running down the track and leaping over the dunes onto the soft, white sand below.

It's late afternoon and there's hardly anyone on the beach, but I can see a couple of fishermen standing out in the surf. Curly is going crazy running up and down the beach, grabbing sticks and bringing them back. Dad throws them way down the beach and Curly charges off after

them. Mum and Dad start walking and we follow along behind, but we keep stopping to look at all the interesting stuff that's washed up.

'Hey, check this out,' yells Max. He's found a large piece of coral that is bleached white from the sun.

We're almost in line with the fishermen now and I can see that they

have a bucket sitting up higher on the sand. Chelsea and I have a look to see if there's anything in it. There are some long red worms. They must be going to use them for bait.

'I think they are beachworms, Chelsea. I read about them once. The fishermen drag a rotten fish over the sand to catch them. The worms pop up and they grab them for bait.'

I feel a bit sorry for the worms as they slide around in the bottom of the bucket.

Chelsea looks sad and turns away from them.

'Oh no,' she says. 'Look at this!'

A small tidal creek is flowing back

into the ocean and some little fish are
trapped. They are flipping about in
what is quickly becoming less and less
water.

'We've got to save them!' I gasp,
looking around for something to put
them in. There are far too many to
carry in our hands and we would drop
them on the sand.

I see the fishermen's bucket and
wonder if they would mind us using it.
It's an emergency, after all!

I run down to the water's edge
and try to call out to them. The wind
throws the noise of the waves and
my calls back into my face and the
fishermen don't turn around.

Chelsea looks really worried when I run back up to her. I can see she's getting upset.

'Juliet, I think they'll die if we don't get them to the water very soon.'

'We'll have to take the bucket and get some water,' I say, grabbing it and racing down to the surf. Mum and Dad and Max are way up the beach now, and we don't have time to get them.

We get to the water's edge, and I gently tip the bucket to the side to let some more water in. The bucket is now a quarter full and already the worms look a lot happier.

'Just a bit more,' I say, tilting the bucket forward just as a huge wave hits. The bucket is bowled over with us and I look up just in time to see the worms happily heading off in every direction.

'Whoops!' We look out at the fishermen who still have their backs to us.

'Perhaps if we put the bucket back when we're finished they won't even notice?' giggles Chelsea, and we grab it and race up the beach.

We quickly scoop each and every little fish into the bucket of water. They dart around looking for a way to escape.

'It's okay,' I say soothingly. 'We're going to save you.'

We lug the bucket to the sea then slowly tip it. The tiny fish leap into the ocean.

'There,' says Chelsea. 'Already it was worth coming camping.'

We put the bucket back where it

was and charge up the beach to tell
Mum. We leave out the bit about the
worms.

Curly runs up and tries to pass
Dad his most recent treasure – a dead
mullet.

'Oh that is gross!' laughs Max.

The fish has been dead for a while
and is stiff from the sun, but Curly
is overjoyed by his find. He keeps
pushing it into Dad's leg to get him
to throw it.

'Yuck, no, Curly!' Dad yells as the
dog chases him around on the sand.
Dad grabs the fish by the tail and
hurls it into the ocean. Curly starts
to whine and looks out to sea, but his

treasure is lost in the waves. Curly looks very sad.

Dad is now rubbing his hands in the sand, trying to get the smell off his fingers. He keeps sniffing them and pulling faces that make Max laugh even more.

We turn around and head back for camp. I can't wait to light the fire and start toasting our marshmallows. Up ahead we can see the fishermen coming out of the surf and heading towards their bucket.

Chelsea and I look at each other.

'Wow! Look at this shell, Mum!' I say.

'And this one, Mr Fletcher,' says Chelsea.

We keep Mum and Dad occupied for a while and glance up at the men. One is peering into the bucket and the other is scratching his head and looking around on the sand. After a while they pick up the bucket and head off.

'We can look for more shells tomorrow,' says Mum. 'It's time to go up for a shower now.'

Chelsea and I race ahead.

On the way, Chelsea and I hear something that sounds really big in the long grass beside the path.

'What's that?' said Chelsea, grabbing my arm.

I try to sound very scientific and

brave, but the noise does sound like something big.

'It's probably just a feral cat or something. I've got a page about them in my Vet Diary,' I say, and we both sprint for the safety of the camping ground.

CHAPTER 3

Vets can't be afraid of the dark

'Honey, what happened to those leftover sausages that were beside the barbecue?' Dad looks at Curly suspiciously. Curly wags his tail. Dad shakes his head.

'That's odd,' says Mum. 'Curly has been sitting here with me the whole time. You'd think we would have seen him. Perhaps it was a kookaburra?'

We all look up into the trees as the sun begins to set. Dad is not convinced.

'Can we light the fire now?' I ask.

❖

'Toasted marshmallows are the yummiest things I've ever eaten,' says Max, licking sticky goo off his fingers as we all sit around the fire a little while later. The warmth on our faces and the way the flames flick up into the air makes me feel all cosy and happy.

'That might do you for tonight, Max,' says Mum, as he reaches for another marshmallow, 'or you might be sick again.'

We go and clean our teeth then crawl into our sleeping bags. I'm exhausted and fall straight to sleep, but not for long.

As soon as Mum and Dad lie down, Curly starts to bark. He isn't used to the sounds of the bush. Dad snaps at him to be quiet, but he doesn't stop.

Dad unzips our side of the tent and comes in. '*Oww!*' he yelps, as he steps on one of Max's dinosaurs.

'I told him not to put them there,' I say, 'but he never listens.' I shine the torch on Max. He's asleep with a dinosaur sitting on his chest.

We finally get Curly to settle down, and I drift back into a deep sleep.

❖

'Juliet, wake up!' Chelsea has the torch shining in my face and she's shaking my shoulder. 'Wake up. I can hear something and so can Curly.'

I rub my eyes and try to focus.

'What?'

'I can hear something outside the tent. There's something moving around out there.'

I look over at Curly. His ears are pricked up and he's growling in a low, deep rumble. I pat him and try

to calm him down so he doesn't start
barking again.

The reflection of the torch on the
sides of the tent makes Chelsea's eyes
look huge and very worried.

'It's fine, Chelsea. I'll go and have
a look.'

'No!' she yelps, grabbing my arm.
'I've been thinking about this. We
heard something big in the grass
today, now some meat has gone
missing so . . . there is something big
out there that eats meat! Juliet . . . it
might eat you!'

Chelsea's lip starts to quiver and
she looks a bit teary. I consider waking
my mum, but vets have to be brave

sometimes, so I decide to unzip the tent just a tiny bit to see if I can see anything.

Curly, as usual, is very enthusiastic. He tries to shove his nose through the small space and starts sniffing like mad. It takes all my strength to pull his head back out of the hole. 'Can you hold onto him, Chelsea? The last thing we need is him waking Dad up.'

I lie down on my stomach and peer out through the gap. I can't see anything at first, but then a movement catches my eye. There *is* something out there!

'Can you see it?' Chelsea's croaky whisper makes me jump. Curly licks

my ear. I hold up my hand in a stop
sign and take another minute to look.
I grab the torch and shine it in the
direction of the movement, and then I
see it!

I turn to Chelsea and put my finger
to my lips, then I slowly unzip the tent
and start to crawl out quietly. Curly
squeezes out beside me. Chelsea is
still holding onto his collar. Dogs are
not very patient at times. I must write
that in my Vet Diary later.

We finally all manage to squeeze
out of the tent and I shine the torch
up into the tree beside our camp
site. There, huddled on a branch and
peering down at us, is a ring-tailed

possum with a gorgeous joey next to
her. The three of us sit quietly and
watch them watching us. Curly's used
to possums, because we raised some
babies in our home after a big bushfire.

I sweep the beam of light around
the other branches, looking to see what
other nocturnal animals are around.

'Look at that!' Chelsea points to a branch up higher. There is a large owl sitting on it and staring down at us.

'That's a barn owl!' I say.

'How do you know?'

'I can tell from its heart-shaped face and the creamy underparts, and those black spots on its wings. They're common all over Australia and eat small rats and mice. That's why they like campgrounds. People leave food around, so rats and mice come.'

'You really are nearly a vet, aren't you?' sighs Chelsea. 'But can we go back to bed now ... before the rats and mice turn up?'

CHAPTER 4

Vets need to teach others

We're all a bit tired the next morning. There were so many different sounds outside our tent last night that poor Curly just couldn't relax and spent most of the night barking to protect us. Dad says Curly's the one that's going to need protection if he barks like that again.

But nothing can spoil our mood as we head to the beach for a swim after breakfast, then on to explore the rock pools. They are crystal clear and

filled with life. Each one is like a little
garden underwater. We see starfish,
crabs and colourful little fish darting
from one rock to another. If you sit
really still without your shadow over
a rock pool, after a while, all the
creatures come out from their hiding
spots. Chelsea and I sit for ages near

one with Mum and she helps us add
more creatures to our list.

ROCK POOL CREATURES:

Fish
Crabs
Sea anemones
Starfish
Oysters
Coral (and I thought it was a plant!)
Sponges
Flat worms
Shrimp

'Yuuuuucccccck! What is that?' Max and
Dad have headed closer to the sea on
their rock pool exploration. 'It looks like
a giant underwater sausage!' says Max.

Mum, Chelsea and I hurry over to them to see what it is.

Mum laughs when she sees what all the fuss is about. 'It's a sea cucumber, Max. Look, you can pick them up.' She reaches in and carefully lifts the soft, brown, cucumber-like creature from the water. Curly sniffs at it curiously. As he does, it squirts long strands of white, sticky glue from one end. We all scream and jump back. Curly barks at it.

'In some countries they eat these as a special treat,' says Dad, and Mum nods in agreement.

I glance over at Chelsea who looks a little pale and is backing away.

'We're not going to eat it, are we Mr Fletcher?'

'Of course not, Chelsea,' I laugh, 'but this guy is getting his own page in my Vet Diary!'

SEA CUCUMBERS:

- Sea cucumbers are the rubbish collectors of the sea – they clean the surface of the sand as they move along.

- There are 1,250 known species.

- When threatened, sea cucumbers discharge sticky threads.

- They are eaten by lots of fish and sea creatures, and some humans.

I am still sitting working on my 'sea cucumber' page when I hear a low rattling sort of sound behind me. I look around the rocks, but I can't see where it's coming from. Chelsea is a little way off, still recovering from the thought of people eating sea cucumbers.

'Did you hear that, Chelsea?'

'Yeah, what was it?'

We are both quiet and listen again for the sound between the waves lapping on the rocks.

'It's coming from over there,' says Chelsea, pointing to the shelf of rocks behind me.

We carefully creep towards the sound and find ourselves holding

37

hands as we peer over a large rock.
There, half in a rock pool, is a pelican,
and it's in a lot of trouble!

'Mum! Mum! Come quickly!'

Mum, Dad and Max start to head
towards us as fast as they can across
the slippery rocks. When they reach
us, we all peer over at the very sad
pelican.

'It's caught up in fishing line,' says Dad.

Mum knows what to do straight away. Vets always do.

'Juliet and Chelsea, can you run back to the camp and get some scissors and some beach towels? We'll have to try to cut him free before the tide comes back in.' She looks over at Dad. 'I should have brought my vet kit.'

Chelsea and I look at each other then race off to the camp site.

We are back in no time and, of course, I have my vet kit, my emergency rescue kit, and my pet carrier too – just in case.

Mum slowly slides down the rocks

beside the pelican. He's very frightened
and makes low squawking noises. I
snap open my kit on the rocks above
our patient. We pass Mum the towels.
She's going to have to put them over
the bird's head to keep him calm and
still while we untangle him. Pelicans
are quite big and strong and can give
a nasty bite.

When the towels are on, Dad slides
down to hold the bird still. Chelsea
and I climb down to them and I pass
Mum the scissors from my kit and
some antiseptic cream. Mum smiles at
me. 'Good thinking, Juliet. It's great
that you brought your kit.'

'Well, you just have to when you're

nearly a vet,' replies Chelsea.

Mum carefully snips at the line caught around the pelican while I dab along behind her with some antiseptic cream on a cotton ball where the skin has been broken. Luckily he hasn't been cut too badly, but we got here just in time. Had the tide come in, he would have drowned for sure.

Finally the line is all cut away and Mum tells us to get back up on the rocks. She slowly takes the towel off the pelican and for a minute he just stares at us. Then he flaps his wings madly and jumps to the side. We all back away to give him some more space. The pelican flies about ten metres away then lands and looks back at us. Then he starts to clean himself.

'That's a good sign,' says Mum. 'Really sick animals don't bother to clean themselves.'

I must remember to write that in my Vet Diary.

'What is that smell?' asks Dad, and we all look behind us to see Curly wagging his tail. He's found his mullet and he is very, very happy about it. The mullet is looking a little worse for wear. It's now swollen with bulging eyes.

Dad and Chelsea look like they are going to be sick.

'Phew! It stinks!' laughs Max hysterically.

Mum takes charge. 'Girls, I'll get the fish off Curly and you take him up to the camp and wash around his mouth. Dad and I will bury this fish once and for all.'

'I'll help,' says Max, rushing to get his sandcastle spade.

As we drag Curly back to the camp site we try to cover his eyes so he can't see where the fish is being buried. He is very upset about being parted from his treasure again and struggles to break free. I look back at the beach and see that Max is already waist-deep in a hole and still digging.

'Maybe a bath might calm him down,' Chelsea suggests, and ducks into the tent to get her grooming kit.

In no time at all Chelsea has
Curly in a lovely foamy mass and he
does seem to forget his troubles as
she massages the shampoo into his
back and ears. She rinses and trims,
brushes and fluffs, until Curly looks
like a new dog.

'You really do have a gift, Chelsea,'
I say, and Mum nods in agreement as
she comes up from the beach.

Mum and Dad need a rest so we
hang around the camp site after lunch.
Chelsea and I make some posters for
around the campground to educate
people on the dangers of leaving
fishing line lying around. Education is
all part of a vet's job, you know.

CHAPTER
5

Sometimes vets need
to be a bit sneaky!

After we've finished putting our posters
up, we race down to join Mum, Dad and
Max, who are back at the beach.

There are heaps of people down
there and a lot of them seem to be
doing a funny sort of dance. We can see
Mum and Max doing it, too.

'What are you doing?' I pant when
we get to them.

'Fishing for pipis!' says Max,
proudly holding up his bucket with

a dozen or more smooth brown pods of two shells joined together. 'Watch this!' Max puts a pipi on the wet sand and we stare in amazement as the shell opens slightly, flips up onto its end and starts to twist and bury into the sand.

'You find them by twisting your feet into the wet sand.' Mum shows us the action.

Chelsea and I join in and pretty soon we are adding to Max's collection. I look around and notice the fishermen from yesterday are doing it, too.

'Why is everyone collecting them?' I ask, and stop twisting as soon as I hear the answer.

'Some do it for fun, like us,' says
Mum. 'Other people use them for bait.
They pry the shell open with a knife
and put the pipi on the fishing hook.
Fish love them.'

Chelsea, Max and I look down at
our shiny pipis in the bucket. Max
starts to look a bit upset. 'I don't want
my pipis to die.'

'I have an idea, Max,' I whisper.
'Let's take them up to the beach on
the other side of the rock pools and
let them go there where nobody will
find them.'

We all agree that it's a good plan
and Mum wraps her towel around
the bucket so that people don't notice,

otherwise they might follow us for an easy catch.

Curly is excited and runs ahead. He loves an adventure.

We tip the pipis out and sit around them in a circle as they start to burrow. We are taking turns to guess which one will be the last to disappear when suddenly we are greeted by a familiar smell.

'Oh, no!' laughs Mum. 'He's found his mullet again!'

Sure enough Curly, now covered in wet sand, is holding the treasured mullet in his mouth. Its head is now hanging half off and one eye is missing. He wags his tail at us.

Chelsea lets out a small cry. 'Oh Curly, your beautiful coat is filthy again!'

Mum tries to grab the fish off him, but Curly thinks it's a game. He runs around in happy circles, then takes off up the beach towards our tent. Everyone knows who he's going to give it to!

'Dad!' we all screech and run after him, but we're too late.

We hear Dad's bellow a few moments later. Then we see him chasing Curly around the tent with a rolled-up newspaper. Dad is out of breath when we get there.

'That dog . . .' he says to Mum. 'That *dog* just dropped a rotten, stinking mullet on my bare chest while I was asleep. Why he had to come camping, I will never know!'

Chelsea and I try to block Curly's ears. It's not his fault that he likes to fetch things. He usually gets a pat for it.

Dad makes us tie Curly up while he

puts the dead fish in a plastic bag, and then another, and ties them off. He throws the mullet into the wheelie bin on his way to the shower. Dad's not a huge fan of animals, and especially not dead ones by the looks of it.

Curly lets out a little whimper. He liked that mullet.

CHAPTER 6

Vets are always learning

The next morning we are at the beach early and it's a beautiful day. There are surfers out on their boards and the sun is making the water sparkle. Max and Dad are out swimming when everyone starts to call and point out to sea.

There's a pod of dolphins diving through the waves chasing schools of fish. The surfers are so lucky! They're sitting on their boards right amongst them. I would love to be out there, too.

We watch them for ages and then Chelsea and I go back to building the perfect dinosaur zoo out of sand for the dinosaurs Max has carried down to the beach. Mum is reading her book under the umbrella.

After a while one of the surfers comes up the beach to get his stuff right near Mum.

'You were lucky to be out there amongst the dolphins,' says Mum.

'We sure were,' smiles the surfer. 'I haven't seen that many at one time in ages. It must be all the whitebait that's around. There's some pilot whales out there, too, and one of them has a calf.'

He shakes water from his afro, then he dries himself off and heads up the beach with his board under his arm.

By now Chelsea and I are on our feet again, peering out to sea. 'Pilot whales! I've never seen a real whale, Mum. Will we be able to see them from here?'

'I don't think so,' says Mum. 'They don't tend to come in as far as the dolphins. You know, Juliet, pilot whales are not actually whales. They are the second-largest member of the dolphin family, after killer whales.'

I race to my backpack and whip out my Vet Diary, brushing the sand off my hands as I go. This definitely needs a whole page.

PILOT WHALE FACTS:

- Pilot whales are usually dark black, but sometimes they are grey.

- They mostly eat squid and sometimes eat fish.

- Male pilot whales are about 5 metres long.

- There are two species: the long-finned and the short-finned pilot whale.

- Pilot whales aren't really whales at all! They're a type of dolphin.

We head up for lunch and Chelsea and I go over to the toilet block. Curly follows along, but stops at the wheelie bin area. He sniffs and looks around sadly.

'He really liked that mullet,' says

Chelsea, and she bends down to give him a hug.

'Would you like us to groom you to take your mind off it?' she asks him.

Curly tries to lick her cheek and wags his tail. We guess that means yes.

After lunch we play some board games. Curly is looking very smart because Chelsea and I have brushed his hair into sections and made little pigtails all over him.

'That should keep the knots out for a while, anyway,' says Chelsea, leaning over to pat him. Curly seems to be very interested in Max this afternoon. He keeps sniffing around him and laying his head on his lap.

'He just loves me,' laughs Max, as Curly burrows his nose into him again.

Chelsea, Max, Curly and I decide to head back down to the rock pools and hunt for some more sea cucumbers. Mum and Dad sit up at the top of the beach to keep an eye on us.

We find eight sea cucumbers and put them all in one rock pool and start giving them names. I grab my Vet Diary to keep a list so we don't forget them all.

SEA CUCUMBER NAMES:
Chubby
Stretchy
Sticky
Slimy
Blobby
Longy
Stinky (Max named that one)
Bendy

They are the funniest things I have ever felt. They are like long, water-filled balloons that go all floppy when you pick them up. We carry them gently so they don't squirt their glue out because it's really gross and sticky.

Eventually we put our 'pet cucumbers' back where we got them from and head up the beach to Mum and Dad. Then we all head back to the camp site.

Curly runs ahead of us and starts barking like mad when he gets there.

'You guys wait here a minute,' says Dad. He and Mum go ahead to look.

CHAPTER 7

Vets need to know how to follow a trail

'It's okay,' calls Mum after a minute or so. 'You can come now.'

Our camp site is a mess. The plastic bag that held our rubbish has been ripped open and garbage is spread out everywhere.

'Something's got into the garbage,' says Dad. He looks over at Curly.

'Unless Curly has grown some very sharp claws, and leaves rather odd tracks in the sand. I think he's innocent,' says Mum. 'What we have here is the leftovers of a goanna's breakfast. Look – you can see the marks from his tail in the sand. It's a big one.'

'I should have put the garbage in the bin,' says Dad. 'I forgot.'

'What's a goanna?' asks Max.

I whip out my Vet Diary ready to take notes.

'Well, Max, a goanna is actually a relative of your favourite animals . . . the dinosaurs.'

I scribble down as many notes as I can while Mum speaks.

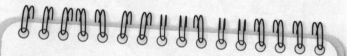

FACTS ABOUT GOANNAS
(also known as monitor lizards):

• They eat meat, including small animals and dead things.

• There are lots of different kinds of goannas and they vary in size. Some grow up to 2m in length.

• They can run fast.

• They can climb trees.

• Goannas can be aggressive if attacked or chased.

I look over at Chelsea. She is now sitting on the table with her legs tucked up, looking around nervously. 'That must have been what we heard the other day in the grass. It could have attacked us!'

'Don't worry, Chelsea. I'm sure it will leave us alone, if we leave it alone.' I look at Mum and she nods.

'And I bet that's what ate all the sausages. Sorry, Curly,' says Dad. Curly wags his tail and looks towards the bin.

'Can we see if we can find it?' says Max. 'I want to see a goanna.'

'I don't,' says Dad. 'Leave it alone.'

'I'll follow the trails with you, Max,' says Mum.

Max runs off to grab some dinosaurs from the tent. 'He might want to meet these guys,' he says.

Chelsea and I roll our eyes.

'Do you want to see if we can find it, Chelsea?'

'Um, you know, I'm a bit tired from last night. I might just pop into the tent and read my book.'

'Okay,' I say. 'We'll call you if we see it.'

Chelsea climbs into the tent and zips it shut. I think she put her bag in front of the zip, too.

Mum, Max and I head off. It's really exciting following the strange trails in the sand, but a bit scary, too. Even vets can be scared of new things.

The tracks disappear when we reach the long grass. We all look around, but it's Mum who spots it. 'There it is!' she whispers, pointing up a large gum tree. 'It *is* a beauty.'

I step a little closer to Mum as I look at the enormous lizard with its long tongue flicking in and out.

I'm glad it wasn't what I saw when I opened the tent that first night!

The goanna's green and black markings help camouflage it in the dappled light coming through the trees.

Max holds each of his dinosaurs up for the goanna to see. He insists on giving a description of each one. The lizard looks totally bored. No surprises there.

Finally we head back to camp for our last night. It has been a lovely holiday and I know so much more about beach animals now. I take a bit of time to finish off some pages in my Vet Diary.

CHAPTER 8

Vets have to be good in an emergency!

The next morning we wake up really early because there's heaps of noise coming from the beach. When we come out of the tent, Dad tells us that Mum is already down there because a pilot whale calf has beached itself.

Oh, no! It's probably the one the surfer was talking about yesterday.

'Mum's just sent up a message for us to bring as many buckets as we can. Take these down with you, girls, and I'll wake Max up.'

We run down to the beach and can't believe our eyes! There is a whale lying on the beach and it can't move. It's so awful I feel like crying. Mum is there and we run to her side with the buckets.

'Quickly, girls, help the other people bring buckets of water up. We have to keep her wet and cool or the heat from the sun will kill her.'

Mum turns to a lady who is watching with one hand over her mouth. Mum is very calm. Vets have to be. 'Could you go and get as many beach umbrellas as you can and towels to put over her?'

The woman is glad to be given

something to do and runs up to the camp site. More and more people are coming with buckets and soon we have a line with buckets being passed from one person to the next and the water is gently poured over the whale.

'Will she be all right, Mum?' I start to feel tight in my throat. 'Is she going to be all right?'

'She's been here since last night when the tide was high,' says Mum. 'Her only chance is if we can keep her cool and wet until the tide comes in this afternoon, and then hope that she can find her mother.'

I feel even sadder knowing it is a baby. Its mother must be frantic.

I look out to sea and start to worry. It's such a big place to look for someone.

The calf blows hard through its blowhole and opens and closes its mouth a few times. Its sad little eye looks up at us.

Chelsea pats her. 'Its going to be okay,' she whispers to the baby whale.

Suddenly the surfer we saw yesterday

appears at Mum's side. He has run all
the way up the beach.

'The pod,' he pants, out of breath.
'They're still out there. We just saw
them. They're still after the whitebait.'

Mum looks relieved. 'How long will
it be until the tide comes back up to
this point?'

'About five hours, I think. It was high

tide around midnight, so it will be high tide again around lunchtime.'

Mum and I look at each other. Vets know what other vets are thinking. That is a long time for the baby whale to stay alive out of the water, and a long time for the pod of pilot whales to stick around. I hope her mother knows we are trying to help.

CHAPTER 9

Sometimes vets need to think fast

Dad brings Mum her mobile phone and she calls Sea World on the Gold Coast and speaks to a marine biologist. He says we are doing everything right. They will try to get here as soon as they can, but they're at least three hours away.

I look at the line of people passing the water. In this heat, they are going to get very tired, very soon. I have an idea and talk it over with Chelsea.

'That's brilliant, Juliet,' she says. 'No wonder you're nearly a vet!'

We make up a roster and go along the line and ask everyone for their name. Then we go up to the camp site and Dad helps us to ask everyone if they could pitch in. If everyone helps, then everyone gets a break, and the baby whale will stay cool and wet until the tide comes back up.

We keep pouring water over the little whale and sheltering her from the hot sun. Every now and then she thrashes about and makes a shrill, panicked sound. I hope her mother can hear her so she doesn't swim away.

Max joins the line of bucket carriers.

I see Mum talking to Dad quietly off to the side. I know she is very worried about the whale.

Ever so slowly, the tide starts to come in. Max uses one of his dinosaurs to mark the highest point a wave reaches each time, and as the scorching sun beats down on us all we wait, and wait, and wait.

By ten o'clock the first wave reaches out from the ocean and touches the whale.

By eleven o'clock we stand around her with the water above our ankles. The whale flips and splashes, but she is still stranded by her weight.

By twelve o'clock it starts to happen.

She starts to be lifted by the waves. The experts from Sea World are here now and the excitement has grown. Our new friend Brett, the surfer, has come back several times to tell us the pod is still out there, and that the mother whale is calling her calf.

'Now,' says the marine biologist to the people gathered around the

three-metre-long baby, 'when the next
wave lifts her, we have to try to push
her into the deeper water. She will
be wonky, so we must try to keep her
upright and pointing into the waves so
she doesn't roll.'

We all hold our breaths and wait for
the next big wave.

'Now,' yells the biologist, and the

whale is pushed forward into the deeper water. The people from Sea World swim out with her and help her through the waves. We are all holding hands and cheering as the little calf slips through the last wave and out to sea.

Brett is waving madly from his board. He signals that the whales are heading in the right direction and he puts his thumbs up when the mother reaches her calf.

The whole beach cheers and every face is smiling.

We stagger up to our camp site and collapse onto the chairs. The people from Sea World are going to stay on for a while, to make sure more whales don't beach themselves.

Mum looks exhausted, but happy. 'Well, you did say you wanted to see a pilot whale, Juliet!'

I look around for Curly to give him a hug. I haven't seen him all morning.

'Dad, where's Curly?'

'I thought he was with you?'

None of us have seen him for ages.

We all start to call out for him.

I start to panic. We were so caught up with the whale that nobody kept an eye on Curly.

'Curly! Curly!' I bellow.

We run around the camp site asking if anyone has seen him. The lady in the tent next door remembers giving him a biscuit around morning tea time, but there are no reports since then.

'Oh where could he be?' I sob.

Max, Chelsea and I are all crying now, and Mum and Dad look really worried too. What a terrible way to end our holiday! First the whale, now this!

A huge garbage truck is coming up the dirt path to collect the wheelie bins. He honks his horn for us to hop off the track. Can't he see we are freaking out? He honks again. I look up to signal for him to stop so I can tell him that our dog is missing. Then I see a very familiar face looking out of the window at me.

It's Curly, still covered in little pigtails.

The driver stops his truck and lifts Curly down. 'Are you looking for this?' he laughs when we run over.

Max, Chelsea and I all hug Curly. He doesn't know who to lick first.

'I saw him in my rear-view mirror following the truck while I collected the bins,' says the driver, 'so I thought I'd better bring him back. With a hairdo like that, he obviously belonged to someone!'

Chelsea looks very proud.

'We should have guessed. He followed the mullet!' says Dad, shaking his head and laughing.

It takes ages to pack all the gear up and sweep the sand out of the tent.

When we are finally finished we all go down to the beach for one last swim. As I jump in the waves I look out to sea and smile at the thought of the whale calf back with its mother.

'You know,' says Dad, when we are back in the car and driving home, 'I'm sure I can still smell that dead fish.'

Mum shakes her head and smiles.

Chelsea and I give Curly a hug.

Max puts his hand in his pocket and pulls out a pet pipi he's been saving from two days ago.

Curly barks excitedly as the smell fills the car.

Quiz! Are You Nearly a Vet?

1. **To find a pipi on the beach, you should:**
a. Call it loudly
b. Look behind your ears
c. Twist your feet in the sand
d. Use a magnifying glass

2. **A mullet is a type of:**
a. Fishing rod
b. Crab
c. Fish
d. Shell

3. **Fishing line left behind is very dangerous for:**
a. Birds and sea life
b. Skipping
c. Fishermen
d. Boats

4. **Nocturnal animals:**
a. Sleep all night
b. Sleep during the day
c. Never sleep
d. Sleep upside down

5. **Which of these is not a type of dolphin?**
a. Spinner
b. Pilot whale
c. Bottlenose
d. Jelly belly

6. A possum is a type of:
a. Reptile
b. Guinea pig
c. Bird
d. Mammal

7. What does a sea cucumber do to protect itself from predators?
a. Hide
b. Shoot out sticky glue
c. Hide in a salad
d. Tie itself in Knots

8. Which bird would be most likely to eat sausages?
a. A budgie
b. A dove
c. A peacock
d. A kookaburra

9. Which is the goanna track?

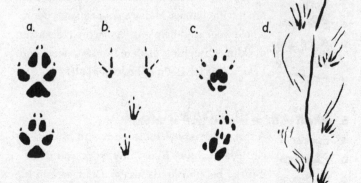

a.   b.   c.   d.

Answers : 1c, 2c, 3a, 4b, 5d, 6d, 7b, 8d, 9d. Well done!

Collect all the **Juliet** *nearly a* **Vet** books!

The Great Pet Plan

My best friend Chelsea and I ♥ animals.
I have a dog Curly and two guinea pigs, but
we need more pets if I'm going to learn to be
a vet. Today, we had the best idea ever...
We're going to have a pet sleepover!

At the Show

Chelsea and I are helping our friend, Maisy,
get her pony ready for the local show. But
Midgie is more interested in eating than in
learning to jump (sigh). Pony training is a bit
more difficult than we thought!

Farm Friends

It's Spring and all the animals on Maisy's farm
are having babies. Maisy says I can stay for a
whole week and help out. There are chicks and
ducklings hatching, orphan lambs to feed, and
I can't wait for Bella to have her calf!

Bush Baby Rescue

A terrible bushfire has struck and Mum's vet
clinic is in chaos. Every day more and more
injured baby animals arrive. Chelsea and I
have never been busier! But who knew that
babies needed so much feeding. I may never
sleep again!